BY MARY LEE DONOVAN · ILLUSTRATED BY BRIZIDA MAGRO

# Let Me
# Call You
# Sweetheart

## A Confectionery of Affection

GREENWILLOW BOOKS, *An Imprint of HarperCollinsPublishers*

Mi cielito,
my angel,
   my moon and my sun—

I call out your name
   with my heart, little one.

Carinho or anjinho—
you're all that,
you're divine.

Stellina, your light
makes the universe shine.

A mouse could eat you up,
you're so precious, doudou—

oi yanak,
    my cutie,
my poppet,
my smoo.

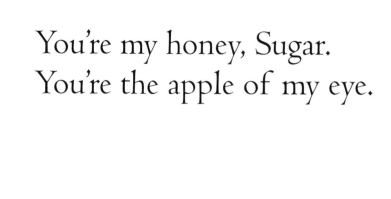

You're my honey, Sugar.
You're the apple of my eye.

A cupcake,
a cream puff,
a real sweetie pie.

Hey, pumpkin.
Hello, puddin',
little dumpling,
crevette.

Bambolino,
bear cub,
my bunny,
my pet.

Little sprout
    or little flower;
        a niblet,
    sweet pea.

Fragolino,
 patatino,
cabbage,

bean.

You're a pip.
You're a bread crumb,
a kitten,

a pup!

Little bee,
    little blossom,
bright buttercup—

in all the world
no one's fonder of you, Duck,

than me.

You're a lambkin,
mousekin,
itty bug,
gra mo chree.

Little sparrow,
   pigeon,
   microbino mio,

goose,

butterfly,

jelly bean,
chickie,
ma puce.

Tadpole
or froggy
or minnow
or mite—

my sweetheart, my dearest,
my darling delight.

Treasured, golden,
    cherished and rare—
like tiny mouse teeth.

You are perfect—a pearl,
a soft fuzzy peach.

Silly, heavenly,
delicious or sweet—

every name, best beloved,
says you're precious to me.

# A CONFECTIONERY OF AFFECTION

Chances are, you have your own well-worn terms of endearment for the ones most precious to you. Maybe you'll even find them in this book. Maybe they are entirely unique to you and your family. Maybe, along with all the variations on *dear, darling, sweetheart, cutie,* etc., discovered in the research for this book, your pet name falls into one of these common categories:

| | |
|---|---|
| Celestial | Things smaller than small |
| Sweet | Birds |
| Edible, yummy | Rare, beautiful, admired objects |
| Small | Green and growing things |
| Baby animals | Plump round things |

In some of the Romance languages, suffixes can be added to a noun to denote something diminutive or small—like carinho (little dear) instead of carina (dear).

Some endearments stand in a class by themselves, like honigkuchenpferd (honey cake horse) in German or bumbubúi (belly dweller) in Icelandic.

## SELECTED TRANSLATIONS OR EXPLANATIONS, IN ORDER OF APPEARANCE

**mi cielito:** my little sky (Spanish)

**carinho:** little dear (Portuguese)

**anjinho:** little angel (Portuguese)

**stellina:** little star (Italian)

**a mouse could eat you up:** moosh bokhoradet (may a mouse eat you) (Persian)

**doudou:** cuddly blanket (French)

**oi yanak:** dear child (Kadazan Dusun, spoken in Malaysia)

**poppet:** endearing, sweet child, usually female (British English)

**smoo:** (made-up endearment)

**apple of my eye:** someone or something dearly cherished, often above others (American English)

**crevette:** small shrimp; used to refer to toddlers (French)

**bambolino:** little doll (Italian)

**fragolino:** little strawberry (Italian)

**patatino:** little potato (Italian)

**pip:** seed (British English)

**microbino mio:** my little microbe (Italian)

**gra mo chree:** love of my heart (Americanized version of Irish grá mo chroí)

# SELECTED SOURCES

Ager, Simon. Omniglot—writing systems and languages of the world. Accessed 1 June, 2022. https://omniglot.com/.

Eberhard, David M., Gary F. Simons, and Charles D. Fennig (eds.). 2022. *Ethnologue: Languages of the World.* Twenty-fifth edition. Dallas, TX: SIL International. http://www.ethnologue.com.

Lomas, Tim. *Translating Happiness: A Cross-Cultural Lexicon of Well-Being.* Cambridge, MA: MIT Press, 2018.

To Smoo, circa 1994—M. L. D.

For Todd, Huck, and Ollie—B. M.

The art was created with rolled printmaking inks, cut paper, pastels, and acrylic paint, then assembled digitally.
The text type is Venetian 301 BT.

Library of Congress Cataloging-in-Publication Data is available.

ISBN 978-0-06-301878-5 (hardcover)

22  23 24 25 26  PC/PC 10 9 8 7 6 5 4 3 2 1
First Edition

 Greenwillow Books